To Monkey,
love

To Robot,
love

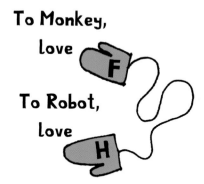

Bloomsbury Publishing, London, Berlin, New York and Sydney

First published in Great Britain in October 2011 by Bloomsbury Publishing Plc
49-51 Bedford Square, London, WC1B 3DP

Text copyright © Felix Hayes 2011
Illustrations copyright © Hannah Broadway 2011
The moral rights of the author and illustrator have been asserted

A CIP catalogue record for this book is available from the British Library

ISBN 978 1 4088 0656 2

All papers used by Bloomsbury Publishing are natural, recyclable products
made from wood grown in well-managed forests. The manufacturing processes
conform to the environmental regulations of the country of origin

Printed in China by Toppan Leefung Printing Ltd, Dongguan, Guangdong

1 3 5 7 9 10 8 6 4 2

www.bloomsbury.com
www.monkeyandrobot.co.uk

Monkey AND **Robot**

In the
Snow

Felix Hayes • Illustrated by **Hannah Broadway**

BLOOMSBURY

LONDON BERLIN NEW YORK SYDNEY

This is Monkey.

'Hi.'

This is Robot.

'Pleased to meet you.'

They are best friends.

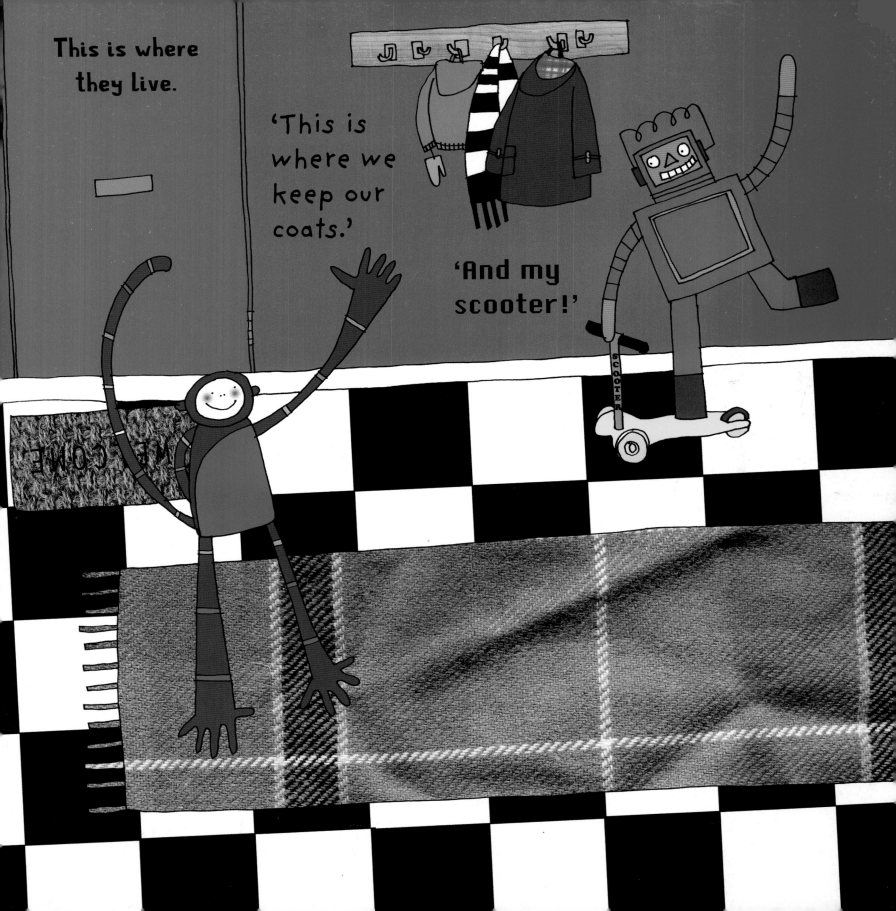

'It's a bit cold,' said Robot.
And he looked out of the window.

'It's all white,'
said Monkey.

'I think it's SNOW!' said Robot.

They put on their coats
and gloves and scarves.

Monkey put on
his wellingtons.

Robot doesn't need
wellies — he has
waterproof feet.

When they got outside it was
freeeezing.

'Brrrrrr.'

Monkey's breath was all frosty.

CREAK,

CREAK,

CREAK,

went Robot's footsteps.

Pong, pong, pong!

Monkey's footsteps
hardly made a sound.

Monkey made
a snow robot.

Robot made a
snow monkey.

Snow Monkey's
head fell off.

'I know! Let's make the biggest snowball ever!' **said Monkey.**

'**OK,**' **said Robot.**

nd he started to roll a snowball.

Soon the snowball was as big as Monkey.

'Bigger,' said Monkey.

So Robot carried on rolling

He rolled it right
out of the garden,

into the park,

around the swings

and past the pond.

The snowball got **bigger** and **bigger** and **bigger**.

Soon the snowball was really big.

'Is it big enough now?' asked Robot.

'Not yet,' said Monkey. 'I'll help.'

Together they rolled . . .

. . . and rolled . . . and rolled.

'**Finished,**'
said Robot.

The snowball was **HUGE!**

'Brilliant,'
said Monkey.

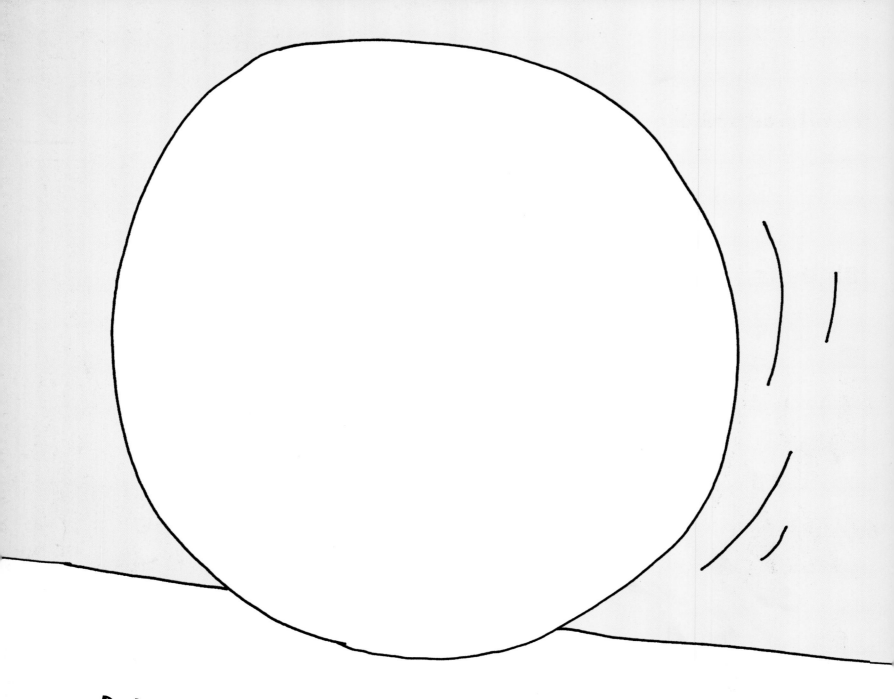

But the giant snowball began to **rumble** and **wobble**.

It teetered and then started to roll.

'Oh dear,' said Robot.

'Run!'
shouted Monkey.

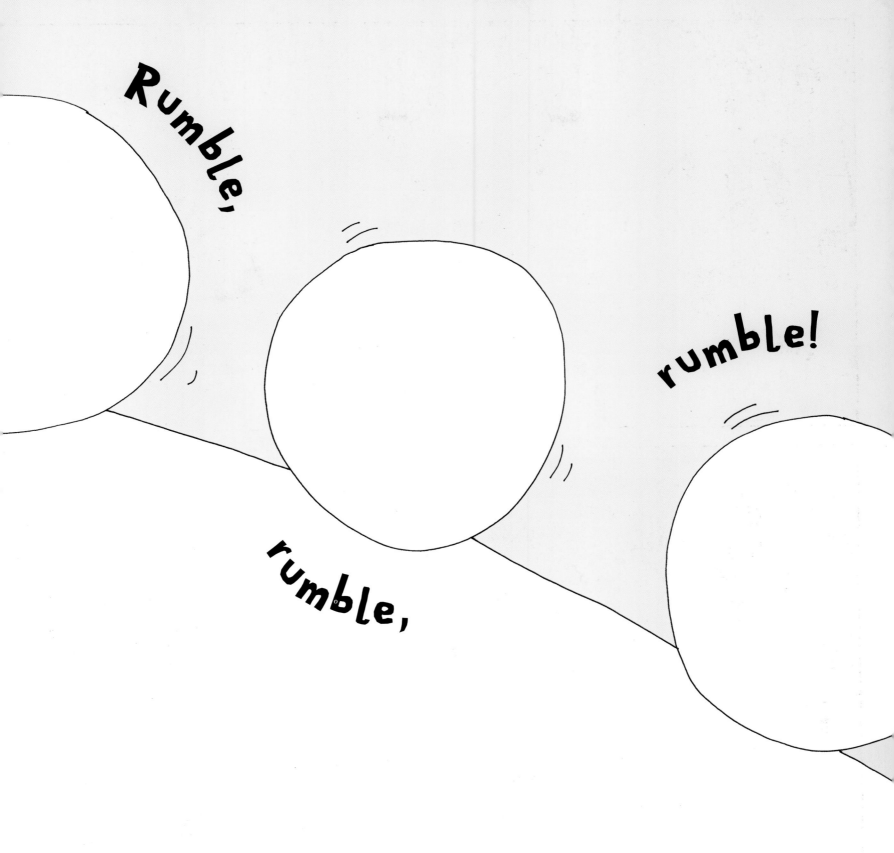

SPLAA

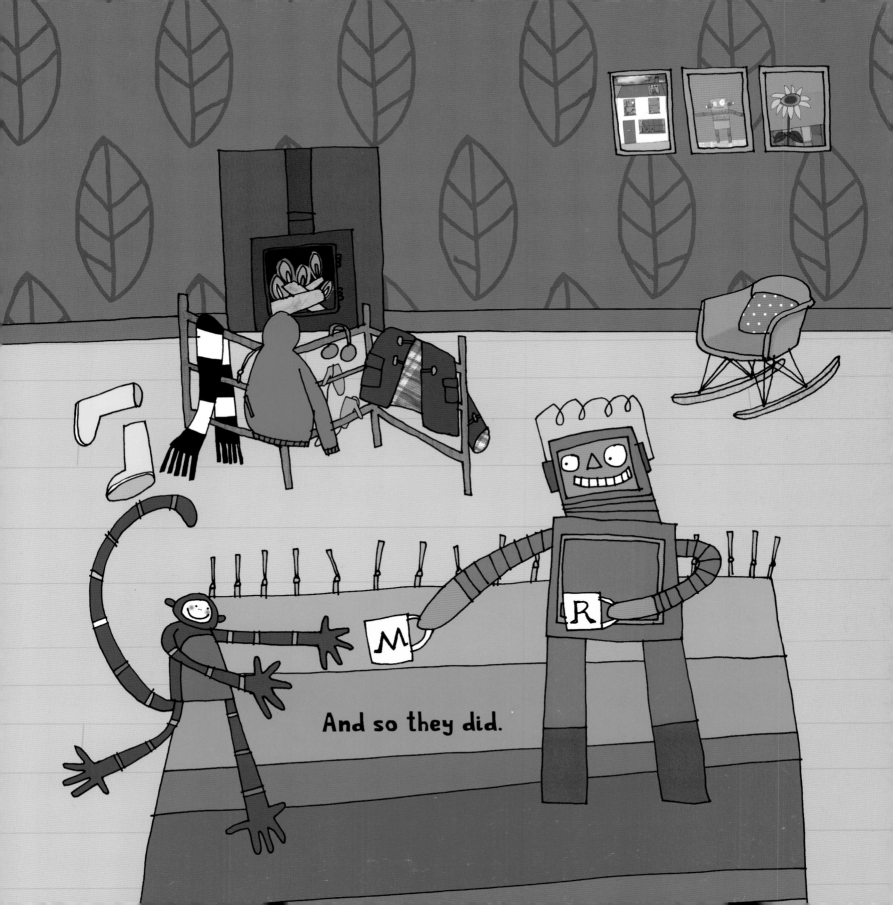

And so they did.

Your Own Snowflakes!

So, unlike lucky Monkey and Robot, there probably isn't any snow outside your window at the moment, is there? But to join in the fun, why not make your own snowflakes? Enjoy making paper snowflakes in lots of different shapes and sizes!

Ask an adult to help you

You will need:

- Plain paper
- A dinner plate
- A pencil
- A small pair of scissors
- Cotton thread
- Blu-tack or magic tape

Directions:

1. Take a piece of plain paper and place a dinner plate upside down in the middle of it

2. With a pencil, draw around the plate so that you have a circle

3. Carefully cut out the circle along the line you've drawn

4. Fold your circle in half

5. Fold the circle in half again so you now have a quarter of a circle

6. Fold the circle in half once more so you now have an eighth of a circle

7. Draw patterns on one side within the eighth of your circle. You can do different designs for each snowflake — that is how to make your snowflakes different!

8. Carefully cut out the shapes with your scissors

9. Carefully open out the circle and there you have your snowflake. It's so easy! If you want, ask an adult to iron the circle to make it totally flat

10. Ask an adult to make a tiny hole at the top of your snowflake, then push some cotton thread through the hole so it can hang up. Or use Blu-tack or magic tape to stick your snowflake to a window so it looks like it's snowing!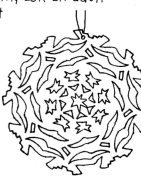

'Hello.'

'Hello.'

To meet **Monkey and Robot**, **play** some **fun games** with them, **find out** about their **adventures** and **lots more**, **go to**

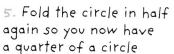

www.monkeyandrobot.co.uk